The GREAT Animal Race

A CHINESE ZODIAC TALE FOR THE LUNAR NEW YEAR

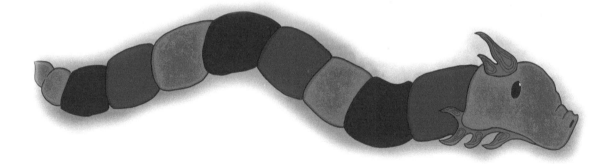

Written by
Paula Zhou

Illustrated by
Jenna Croftcheck

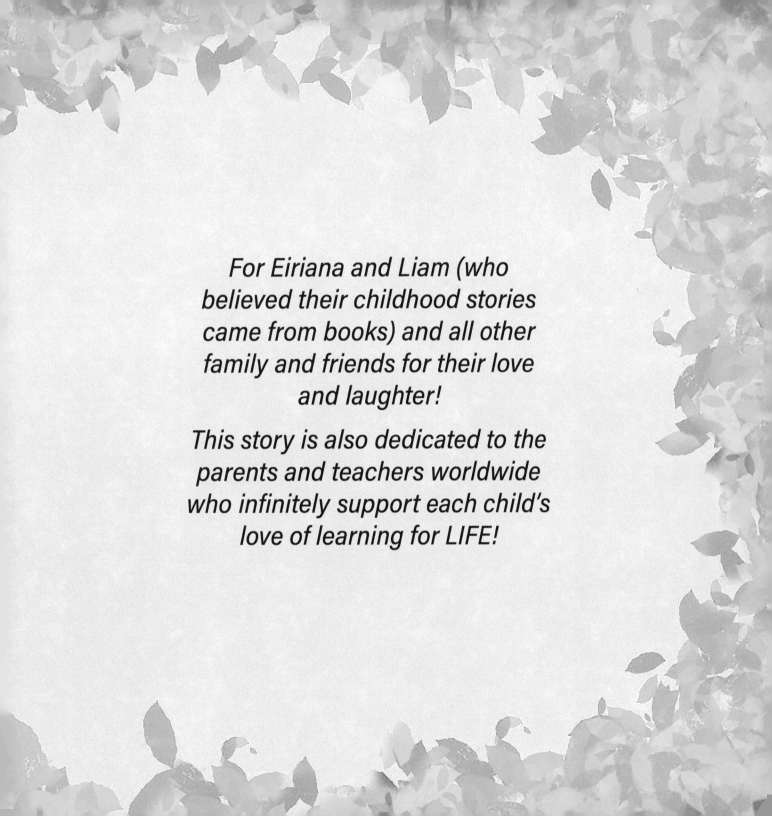

For Eiriana and Liam (who believed their childhood stories came from books) and all other family and friends for their love and laughter!

This story is also dedicated to the parents and teachers worldwide who infinitely support each child's love of learning for LIFE!

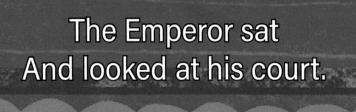

The Emperor sat
And looked at his court.

"Good people," he said,
"I've had a **GREAT** thought!

Every year on my birthday we do the same thing,
And I'm sorry to tell you, but it's **OH-SO-BORING!**
This year, we shall party, dance, and embrace,

And to start it all off...
A great **ANIMAL RACE!**"

"Summon the animals,
All shall attend!
**LET THEM ALL
GATHER,**
At the great river's bend!"

So, the very next day,
No one was late.
Everyone waited,
At the great river's gate.

THE EMPEROR GREETED THE ANIMALS ALL.

He looked so excited; handsome and tall!

He shouted, "**HURRAH**," and off they all dashed,

Into the river with a splish-splashy-splash!

Old **PANDA** sat in a nearby tree,
(She knew she'd be safe in China's history),
Munching bamboo and watching them swim,
Eager to find out, just who would win.

She called out the action
For all to hear.
The **EXCITEMENT** was tense,
The air thick with cheer.

The hard-working **OX**
IS LEADING THE PACK.
But wait, who's that sitting astride on her back?
As the great Ox strode and the water swirled,
Old Ratty and Catty enjoyed the whole world!

You see they let Ox do all the hard work,
With the finish in view, the toil they did shirk.
But **RATTY**, more crafty and gruesome than that,
Did **TRICK** poor old Cat with a fish that was fat.

CAT jumped right in to catch his feast,
While Rat took his place on the nose of the beast!
As they closed in on the finishing line,
Old Ratty jumped off – in the nick of time!

Panda yelled out, "Who's coming next?
IT'S TIGER! He's swimming ahead of the rest!"
So mighty and bold, so brave and so strong;
Tiger makes third to the sound of a gong!

Flying above the crowds,
Look up high;
Majestic and long,
DRAGON swoops by.

But, wait! She drops someone
Before she lands.
Little **RABBIT** bows low
For the helping hand.

The crowd goes wild as **HORSE** draws close,
Her beautiful mane aglow as she goes.
But what just happened as she neared the line?
SNAKE slides from under her hoof, just in time!

That **SNEAKY OLD SNAKE** was hiding there,
Getting ready to startle poor Horse as she neared.
So, in 6th place, Snake, and 7th, Horse;
Getting close to the end of this racing course.

There in the distance old Panda can see,
A boat full of friends playing with glee!
GOAT, **MONKEY**, and **ROOSTER** having such fun!
Rowing their boat to the beat of a drum!

The trio wonders: 8th place, who should claim?
ROCK, PAPER, SCISSORS – the deciding game.

They near the banks and what can we see?
Goat jumps for joy, "Oh Yay! It's ME!"

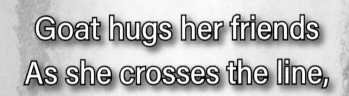

Goat hugs her friends
As she crosses the line,

With Monkey, then Rooster,
Following behind.

The crowd is on pins;
The air thick and tense!
Panda calls out,

"THE EXCITEMENT'S IMMENSE!"

In the distance, a splash and a swirling of waves,
Reveals **LITTLE PUPPY**, enjoying his bathe!
Cavorting and frolicking right to the end,
He **CROSSES THE FINISH** and lopes to his
friends.

ELEVEN animals,
ALL ON DRY LAND!
The emperor, elated,
Raises his hands!

As everyone cheers
And heads for the vans,

A splashing is heard
As old **PIG COMES TO LAND.**

PANDA calls out,
"The race is complete,
Enjoy yourselves friends;

DANCE,

SING,

and EAT!"

And that is the story of how it began:
The **EMPEROR**, the **RACE**, and the
ZODIAC PLAN.

Now each **LUNAR NEW YEAR,**
(The New Year of the Moon)
TWELVE ANIMALS take turns
To bring **LUCK AND FORTUNE.**

The **YEAR YOU WERE BORN**
Is your **ANIMAL YEAR.**
Mine is the Rabbit!
WHAT'S YOURS? Write it here!

---

*You will note that the **cat** is missing on the Zodiac.
Remember that the cat was tricked by the rat and left the race...
Hence the feud between cat and rat continues!

Jenna Croftcheck, Illustrator

Jenna Croftcheck works with Oprelle Publications as a Team Coach and their Artistic Director.

She is an award-winning artist, animal rights proponent, and lover of our planet. She is currently studying Psychology at the University of Boulder, Colorado.

Jenna not only keeps us all in check, but also helps to personally illustrate all genres of book covers as well as picture books in our Oprelle Kids Imprint. We are so happy to have Jenna's talent and steady in a chaotic world.

Paula Zhou, Author

Originally from a small town in the Welsh valleys, Paula has lived in China working in early years education since 1998.

Discovering her 'animal' was one of the very first things that she did when she landed in 'The Middle Kingdom', and exploring folk tales, immersing herself in both the language and 5000-year-old culture, is still a favourite pastime!

The Great Animal Race has been told and retold a thousand times in a thousand different ways. Aimed at children from 3-108, Paula adds a pinch of pizzazz to this age-old story with fun characters who slide through the book on a roller-coaster of rhythm and rhyme!

CPSIA information can be obtained
at www.ICGtesting.com
Printed in the USA
BVHW012329090223
658265BV00022B/387